JoJo and the Eagle

by Peter Rosnick

illustrated by Kathryn Burke

2

Other Books in the JoJo Series

JoJo and the Lion – First told by Chick Rosnick circa 1950
Transcribed by Peter Rosnick and
Illustrated by Samantha Crawford – 1992

JoJo and the Gazork – Written by Peter Rosnick;
Illustrated by Kathryn Burke - 2022

In the Works

JoJo at the Llama Ranch

JoJo, the Firefighter

JoJo, who is only as big as a grandfathers's thumb, was walking around the lake with his good friends The Gazork and the Friendly Lion. They remembered how JoJo saved the Gazork from her own sneeze and saved the lion when he fell into a giant hole.

I'm sure you are asking: How can JoJo, who is only as big as a grandfather's thumb, help these giant beings?

I'll tell you. It is because JoJo is smart, clever, thoughtful, and brave.

What a beautiful day it was. So beautiful that when the Gazork and the Lion said they needed to get home, JoJo said that he would stay and make another loop around the lake.

Oh, the wonders he could see!

He saw small things

like the orange newt

like the iridescent hummingbird

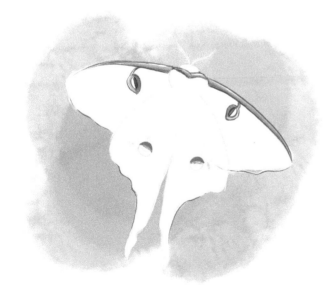

like the greenish blue Luna moth.

He saw medium sized things

like the bull frog catching flies

like the fox and her kits

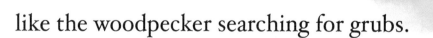

like the woodpecker searching for grubs.

And he saw large things

like a bear munching blueberries

like a black and bronze Water Snake

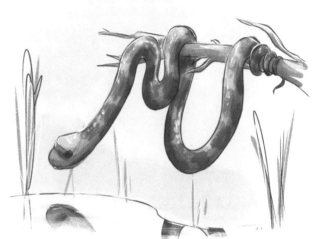

like a tremendous moose dripping
from an underwater plunge.

9

And he heard wonderful sounds

he heard the calls from the Bluebird and the Goldfinch and the Scarlet Tanager

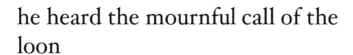

he heard the mournful call of the loon

and he heard a long, high pitched screech from far above his head.

What made that last sound? There it was, again. And again. He searched the skies, but couldn't see anything.

Again the call. This time, JoJo saw the tiniest dot, way up high in the sky.
Again the screech and JoJo could see the dot was a bird soaring on fully spread wings.

And it was getting closer.

Screech! Screech! Now JoJo saw the white head, the dangling talons.

Screech! Screech. Now JoJo thought he could see the Eagle's cycs and it seemed as though the eyes were looking straight at him.

Screech, screech! Before you could say American Bald Eagle three times, JoJo was scooped up by the bird's talons and they were flying away.

Now JoJo had gotten himself in a lot of pickles before, but this time seemed like the worst pickle of all. It seemed like he was in an impossible pickle; the pickle of all pickles.

Nevertheless, JoJo did the thing he always did when he had a problem to solve:
He thought.... And he thought.... And he thought.... And he got an idea!

He decided he would have a conversation with the Eagle.

"Hello, Ms. Eagle. My name is JoJo. It's nice to meet you."
"It's nice to meet you too, JoJo."

"May I ask where you are taking me?"
"Of course. I'm taking you to my nest to feed you to my chicks."

Quite the pickle was JoJo in! And so,
He thought... And he thought... And he thought..., And he got an idea.

He said to the Eagle: "I don't think that is a very good idea – for three reasons."
"I'm listening", said the Eagle.

"First, I am very small. I wouldn't provide much nourishment for your chicks".

This did not persuade the Eagle. She hunted all day and often gave her chicks small amounts at a time.

"Second", said JoJo, "People tell me that I am smart, clever, thoughtful, and brave. Someday, I will be able to help you."
The Eagle stifled a laugh with this idea. She didn't want to hurt JoJo's feelings, but really! How could JoJo, who is only as big as a grandfather's thumb, help a being as large as an Eagle?
JoJo continued; "Third, I had pickle and Jalapeño pepper pizza for lunch, so I don't think I would taste very good."
Now, the Eagle was convinced. She had eaten a Jalapeño pepper before and her mouth was on fire for hours. The thought of combining that with pickles was too much. And so, she dropped JoJo off where she had picked him up, saying; "I hope you have a good rest of your day, JoJo."

"Thank you," replied JoJo. "You, too. And remember, if ever you are in trouble, call for me to help you."

The Eagle just smiled and flew away.

Well, the very next day, JoJo was watching the weather and a tremendous thunderstorm was headed directly towards the tree in which the Eagle had built her nest.

JoJo knew he needed to act quickly to warn the Eagle. He ran as fast, as fast, as fast as he could go (which was VERY fast) to the Eagle's tree. He called up to her and said;

"You have to get your chicks to safety. I'll keep your nest safe".

And so, Ms. Eagle flew with her chicks to her cousin's nest in the next town.

But how was JoJo going to protect her nest? Just then, a boom of thunder sounded; the wind began to blow. JoJo had no time to lose. And so,

He thought... And he thought... And he thought..., And he got an idea.

JoJo ran as fast, as fast, as fast as he could go
(which was VERY fast) back to his house and
picked up rope.
But he knew it wasn't enough rope.

Another flash of lightning and very loud
thunder. The wind was blowing harder. So,
JoJo ran as fast, as fast, as fast as he could go
(which was VERY fast) from one house to the
next gathering many, many pieces of rope.

More lightning. Louder thunder. Stronger wind.

JoJo tied all of the pieces of rope together making a VERY long
piece of rope. And he ran as fast, as fast, as fast as he could go
(which was VERY fast) back to the Eagle's nest.

JoJo climbed with the rope as fast, as fast, as fast as he could climb (which was VERY fast) to the top of the tree. Holding one end of the rope, he clambered around and around the nest, over and over again, With the nest now completely wrapped in rope, JoJo took the other end of the rope, and jumped off of the nest.

Now, I'm sure you are wondering: was JoJo crazy? Why would he jump from the tallest tree by the lake in this horrifying thunderstorm?

But no, JoJo wasn't crazy. Because, he had thought, and thought, and thought.... And had gotten an idea. JoJo knew that if he jumped in the direction the wind was blowing, the rope and he together would act like a kite. And sure enough, the wind pushed JoJo and the rope such that he landed next to a sturdy tree.

Quickly, JoJo tied the rope around the base. And though the nest still swayed in the wind, it could no longer be destroyed.

Once again, JoJo had saved the day.

The Eagle returned with her chicks when the storm had ended. Imagine her surprise to see how JoJo had protected the nest. She was overjoyed and wrapped JoJo in her wings with the warmest hug.

"JoJo," she said. "The people are right. You are smart, clever, thoughtful, and brave. I never should have doubted you. Please let me know if there is ever a way I can repay you."

I bet you are wondering if that is the end of the story. Well it is, and it isn't. Because the Eagle does help JoJo one day. To find out how, we'll just have to read *JoJo at the Llama Ranch* together.

I really look forward to doing that with you soon.

THE (kind of) END. . .

JOJO AT THE LLAMA RANCH

Printed in the USA
CPSIA information can be obtained
at www.ICGtesting.com
BVHW012225150823
668611BV00002B/2